P9-EAI-886

WHEN I WAS YOUNG IN THE MOUNTAINS

by Cynthia Rylant

illustrated by Diane Goode

E. P. DUTTON · NEW YORK

KRAXBERGER SCHOOL LIBRARY

FIC
RYL
19210

Text copyright © 1982 by Cynthia Rylant
Illustrations copyright © 1982 by Diane Goode
All rights reserved.

Unicorn is a registered trademark of E. P. Dutton

Library of Congress number 81-5359
ISBN 0-525-44198-0

Published in the United States by E. P. Dutton,
a division of Penguin Books USA Inc.

Published simultaneously in Canada by
Fitzhenry & Whiteside Limited, Toronto

Editor: Ann Durell Designer: Riki Levinson

Printed in Hong Kong by South China Printing Co.
First Unicorn Edition 1985 W
12 11 10 9 8

for my grandparents, Elda and Ferrell Rylant

C. R.

for Nicole and Christopher Capuozzo

D. G.

When I was young in the mountains, Grandfather came home in the evening covered with the black dust of a coal mine. Only his lips were clean, and he used them to kiss the top of my head.

When I was young in the mountains,
Grandmother spread the table with hot
corn bread, pinto beans and fried okra.

Later, in the middle of the night,
she walked through the grass with me to the
johnny-house and held my hand in the dark.
I promised never to eat more than one serving
of okra again.

When I was young in the mountains,
we walked across the cow pasture and through the woods, carrying our towels. The swimming hole was dark and muddy, and we sometimes saw snakes, but we jumped in anyway.

On our way home, we stopped at
Mr. Crawford's for a mound of white butter.
Mr. Crawford and Mrs. Crawford looked
alike and always smelled of sweet milk.

CORN STARCH
COMPRESSED
COOKED
CORNED BEEF
PURE
DR PRICE'S
CREAM
BAKING
POWDER
POTTED
HAM
1 gal.
MASON
COCOA
CIGARS

When I was young in the mountains,
we pumped pails of water from the well at
the bottom of the hill, and heated the water
to fill round tin tubs for our baths.

KRAXBERGER SCHOOL LIBRARY

Afterward we stood in front of the
old black stove, shivering and giggling,
while Grandmother heated cocoa on top.

When I was young in the mountains,
we went to church in the schoolhouse
on Sundays, and sometimes walked with the
congregation through the cow pasture
to the dark swimming hole, for baptisms.

My cousin Peter was laid back into the water, and his white shirt stuck to him, and my Grandmother cried.

When I was young in the mountains,
we listened to frogs sing at dusk and awoke
to cowbells outside our windows. Sometimes
a black snake came in the yard, and my
Grandmother would threaten it with a hoe.

If it did not leave, she used the hoe
to kill it. Four of us once draped a very
long snake, dead of course, across our necks
for a photograph.

N.L. ELLIS
TRAVELING
PHOTOGRAPH

When I was young in the mountains,
we sat on the porch swing in the evenings,
and Grandfather sharpened my pencils with his
pocketknife. Grandmother sometimes shelled
beans and sometimes braided my hair. The dogs
lay around us, and the stars sparkled in the sky.
A bobwhite whistled in the forest.
Bob-bob-bobwhite!

When I was young in the mountains,
I never wanted to go to the ocean, and I never
wanted to go to the desert. I never wanted
to go anywhere else in the world, for I was
in the mountains. And that was always enough.

KRAXBERGER SCHOOL LIBRARY